new socks

LITTLE, BROWN AND COMPANY
New York — Boston

by bob shea

Notice anything different about me?

Nope, it's not my glasses.

I got New Socks!

These New Socks fit just right!

Orange must be my size!

Not really!
I just like orange.

Wood Floor!

Whoa!

Look out!
New Socks are just warming up!

Watch me not be scared on the big-kids slide!

In New Socks!

HA! Watch this!

In New Socks!

**Briiiiinnng...
Briiiiinnng...**

Hello, Leon here.
Oh, hello Mr. President!
New Socks?
Yes, you heard correctly.
This afternoon?
Why yes, I do believe
we're free.

Did you hear that, New Socks?
We're going to meet the president!

What can't these New Socks do?

Now I'm all excited to get pants!

For my mother
— Bob

Little, Brown and Company
Hachette Book Group USA
1271 Avenue of the Americas, New York, NY 10020
Visit our Web site at www.lb-kids.com

First Edition: April 2007

Library of Congress Cataloging-in-Publication Data

Shea, Bob.
New socks / by Bob Shea. — 1st ed.
p. cm.
Summary: A chicken is filled with excitement and
self-confidence when he dons a new pair of orange socks.
ISBN-13: 978-0-316-01357-4
ISBN-10: 0-316-01357-9
[1. Socks—Fiction. 2. Chickens—Fiction.] I. Title.
PZ7.S53743Ne 2007
[E]—dc22
2006013741

10 9 8 7 6 5 4 3 2 1

SC

Manufactured in China